The Magic Hockey Skates

story by
Allen Morgan

pictures by
Michael Martchenko

Stoddart
Kids

*We acknowledge the Canada Council for the Arts and the
Ontario Arts Council for their support of our publishing program.*

First published in 1991 by Oxford University Press

Published in 1994 by Stoddart Publishing Co. Limited

Published in Canada by
Stoddart Kids,
a division of Stoddart Publishing Co. Limited
34 Lesmill Road
Toronto, ON M3B 2T6
Tel (416) 445-3333 Fax (416) 445-5967
E-mail Customer.Service@ccmailgw.genpub.com

Distributed in Canada by
General Distribution Services
325 Humber College Blvd.,
Toronto, ON M9W 7C3
Tel (416) 213-1919   Fax (416) 213-1917
E-mail Customer.Service@ccmailgw.genpub.com

Published in the United States by
Stoddart Kids,
a division of Stoddart Publishing Co. Limited
180 Varick Street, 9th Floor
New York, New York 10014
Toll free 1-800-805-1083
E-mail gdsinc@genpub.com

Distributed in the United States by
General Distribution Services
85 River Rock Drive, Suite 202
Buffalo, New York 14207
Toll free 1-800-805-1083
E-mail gdsinc@genpub.com

Reprinted in 1999

Canadian Cataloguing in Publication Data
Morgan, Allen, 1946–
The magic hockey skates

ISBN 0-7737-5697-3

I. Martchenko, Michael.
II. Title.

PS8576.075M35 1994   jC813'.54   C94-932023-4
PZ7.M67Ma 1994

Printed in Hong Kong

One day in December, when fall was all through and the cold winter weather finally returned to freeze the rinks in the parks again, Joey got out his old hockey skates and tried them on.

"They don't fit any more," he told his dad. "I need a new pair."

"It looks like you're growing again," his dad sighed. "I guess we'd better be stopping in at the skate store tomorrow."

"Great," said Joey's brother, Zach. "I can buy a new goalie mask."

Joey had his eye on a new pair of skates he'd seen in the window the week before. But when they arrived at the store the next day, his dad headed straight for the second-hand rack.

"These should do nicely," the salesman said as he helped Joey try them on. "A fine, sturdy pair and the laces are new."

"A good fit, too," Joey's dad agreed. "We'll take them!"

Joey's heart sank. He'd been hoping they wouldn't.

"New skates would fit even better, I bet."

"Your feet are still growing," his dad answered back. "A used pair will do for now."

Joey's dad went to the front to pay. His brother did too, but on the way he gave Joey a nudge and he made a face. Joey looked down at his feet in dismay.

"Zach's right," he muttered. "They're garbage skates."

The salesman heard what Joey said and he smiled in a kindly way.

"I know they don't look like much," he admitted. "But actually, these are the best skates we have. They're magic!"

"Sure," said Joey, but he didn't really think so.
The salesman leaned closer and lowered his voice.

"They've got power!" he whispered. "Real power! Just give them a rub and make a wish. If your wish has anything to do with skating, it's bound to come true. Try it. You'll see!"

Joey's eyes grew wide in spite of himself.

"Anything I want?" he asked.

"Absolutely!" the man whispered back. "Whenever these skates come to someone new, they always have three fresh wishes inside."

Joey tried out his first wish the next day on the rink in the nearby park. His brother Zach wanted to practise with his new goalie mask. None of the other big kids were around, so he asked if Joey could take a few shots, one-on-one.

"I know you're just small and not all that good, but it's only for fun and it's better than nothing," he said.

When Zach wasn't looking, Joey bent down and rubbed his skates. "I wish I could be a better skater," he whispered.

He picked up his stick and went out on the ice. For a while nothing seemed very different at all. He kept losing the puck, he had two major falls and a number of smaller ones too. Then slowly but surely his skating improved. His ankles straightened up, his stride smoothed out and he dipped and he deked and he streaked down the ice like a pro. By the end of the morning he was skating much better than he ever had before.

"Hey, that was great!" Zach told his brother when they went inside for lunch. "Maybe those skates aren't so bad after all."

Joey smiled back. He had to agree that he thought so too.

Joey got better and better each day. He discovered the trick of skating backwards, his shooting was faster, his aim more true. And although the skates were helping him do it, his own self was doing a lot of it too, because he tried very hard and he practised each day. And all the time he was working that way, he thought about what his next wish should be.

He finally knew on Saturday. Some of the big kids from down below King Street came over and challenged the neighbourhood team to the world hockey championships, best out of one. Zach and his friends were eager to play, but they had to find at least one more player to make a full six-man team. Joey stepped forward and said he would try. Zach's friends all laughed.

"We can't use him!" one of them jeered. "He's only a squirt!"

"Hey listen, you guys," Zach replied. "He may only be a little squirt, but he's the biggest little squirt we can get today!"

So, they let Joey play. Just before the game got underway, Zach took his brother aside.

"I'm taking a chance on you, Joey," he said. "I don't know why, I must be out of my head today. Try not to make me look stupid, okay?"

"Don't worry," Joey told him. "My skates are magic!"

"Magic?"

"Sure," said Joey, and he explained how they worked.

"Oh, great," Zach groaned. "Magic skates. I knew I was crazy to let you play. If the other guys ever hear about this, I'm dead."

He put on his mask and went out on the ice. Joey bent down and rubbed his skates. He hoped that they still had some magic inside.

"I wish I could skate like the big kids," he whispered.

And as it turned out, that's exactly what happened. Even though Joey was the smallest one there, no one could touch him at all! He went end to end up and down the rink, stealing and passing the puck. When the game was over the neighbourhood team was the champion of the world and the King Street crew had to slink home in shame. All of Zach's friends were especially pleased with the way Joey had played.

"Way to go, Squirt, you were ace!" they exclaimed. "Come play in our games any time you want. We can always use guys like you."

"You were great," Zach said, as they walked back home. "I didn't know you could skate like that. Who showed you those moves?"

"I told you," said Joey. "It's the skates. They're magic!"

"Yeah, right. I forgot. How many wishes did you say they've got?"

"Three," Joey told him. "But I've already used up two. You do believe that they're magic, don't you?"

"Could be, maybe so," his brother agreed, but he looked at the skates suspiciously. "If they really are magic, you only have one wish left, you know. I hope you save it for something big."

Joey saved his third wish carefully. He waited all winter for just the right thing. Finally, one day in early spring, his chance came along.

His brother's Atom hockey team was playing in the league championships. Joey took his skates to the game that day. He thought he might wish for his brother to win, but he wasn't too sure that the magic would work from all the way up in the stands. He decided to wait and see how the game went.

For a while it went fine. Zach was doing quite well in goal and he stopped lots of shots. By the end of the first period the game was tied at three.

"Maybe they won't even need my help," Joey told himself hopefully. But near the end of the second period, Zach made a diving save. He disappeared under a pile of players, and when they all finally untangled again, Zach stayed down on the ice.

"He's hurt!" Joey gasped.

Joey rushed into the locker room with his mother and dad. They were all very glad when they saw it was only an ankle sprain.

"You'll be fine again in a few days," his dad explained.

What about now? Can't I go back to the game?" Zach asked.

"I don't see how," his dad replied. "It's probably best if you give it a rest. There'll be lots of other games, son."

"Not like this one," Zach said hopelessly. "It's the championship!"

He looked so sad and completely lost that Joey felt sad too. "But his team's depending on him," he said. "The second-string goalie's no good at all. They'll lose the game for sure."

"Maybe it won't be as bad as you think," his mother said.

Unfortunately, she was wrong about that. The crowd gave a cheer. Joey looked out through the locker room door. It was the end of the second period. The score was six to three.

"We're dead," Zach groaned. Then he told his parents they could head back out to the stands again. "Don't worry about me, I'll be okay. I'll watch the rest of the game from here, I guess."

Joey stayed behind. He knew it was time for his third magic wish.

"Don't worry, Zach," he told his brother. "I've got my magic skates with me!"

"So?"

"So put them on," Joey explained. "They still have one wish left, you know. Maybe they'll help you finish the game."

Zach stared down at Joey's skates. They looked very magic. They even glowed. And all in a flash he suddenly knew they could really do wonderful things. But still, even so, they were much too small.

"No way, Joey boy. My feet are too big. The only guy they fit is you. Hey, wait just a minute. That's it!" he cried. "You could wear them yourself, okay?"

"What good would that do?"

"Plenty!" said Zach. "Those skates are magic and they'll work for you. Grab my extra uniform and get dressed fast! You can take my place in goal."

"Take your place? That'll never work!"

"Sure it will," Zach told him. "This is your chance to be big like me. Make the same moves that I always do and play the same as I play. Nothing more. Then the game will end the same way as it would if I hadn't been hurt. You don't need to worry. You'll have on my mask so they won't see your face. No one will ever know!"

The third and final period was about to begin when Joey came out on the ice. The fans gave a cheer and the team skated over to wish him luck. Nobody realized he wasn't Zach. They were so glad to see him they didn't notice his pads were too big, his stick was too heavy and he hardly could see through the slits in his mask. Joey didn't give himself away by talking. He was too scared to say a word. When he reached the crease he bent over and pretended to tighten a lace. But he rubbed the magic skates instead.

"I wish I could play just like Zach," he whispered.

When he straightened up it was time for the face-off. Suddenly, Joey felt very strange. His pads seemed to fit and his stick felt just right. He could see very well through the slits in his mask. He felt bigger and stronger than ever before. But all at once, just as the puck hit the ice, he remembered something not terribly nice. He'd never played goal before in his life!

"I sure hope these skates are still magic," he thought.

They certainly were. They worked perfectly! Whenever a shot was taken on net, Joey was there to block it. The crowd went crazy and so did the team. They got so excited by Joey's great saves they played the best hockey they'd ever played. They shot! They scored! Again and again! The score was soon even at six apiece.

With twenty seconds to go in the game, they faced-off by Joey's goal.

The crowd got up on its feet and clapped. The players were tense. They tried to get ready. Joey got ready too. His team lost the draw and the puck came back all the way to the point. The slapshot that followed was a cannon blast— low, hot and fast, it went straight for the corner. But Joey got there just in time.

Joey slid off to the side of the net and the puck was right there on his stick. His teammates were down, there was nowhere to pass and the seconds were ticking away. There was nothing to do but to do it himself, so Joey took off with the puck on his own. He skated so fast he was only a blur as he flew down the ice.

The crowd began counting the seconds off.

"*Ten . . . nine . . . eight . . . seven . . .*"

With four seconds left Joey reached centre ice and stopped before his skates crossed the line. There was just enough time for one final try, so he drew back his stick and he let the puck fly. His shot was quick and surprisingly tricky. The other team's goalie made a desperate dive, but the puck slid under his outstretched glove and into the net. The siren sounded right after the score. Game over! They won it, seven to six!

The crowd went wild!

While the rest of the team made a victory pile, Joey slipped away to the locker room without being seen. Zach was waiting just inside the door.

"I did it!" Joey laughed, as he gave his brother a very high five. "I told you those skates were magic, didn't I?"

"They certainly were," Zach had to agree. "But if you ask me, you looked like you had lots of magic yourself."

Joey smiled and handed his brother the goalie mask.

"You better get out on the ice," he said, as he unbuckled his pads. "They're about to give out the championship cup."

"But you were the one who won it, not me."

"Not really," said Joey. "You played all year long and made lots of saves. I only played this one part of one game. You'd have done it yourself if you hadn't been hurt. If people are cheering, they're cheering for you."

"No way," said Zach. "I'll tell everyone what really happened."

"Go ahead and try," Joey said with a grin. "Tell them about the magic skates. They'll never believe you, you know."

He gave his brother a great big hug, then pushed him out through the locker room door. Before Zach knew it, his teammates came by and hauled him away out to centre ice to the cries of the cheering fans.

When Joey outgrew his magic skates he put them away in a trunk upstairs. After a while he forgot all about them. Many years later, his mother went up to the attic and discovered them there. She didn't suspect they were magic, of course, so she sent them away to a second-hand store. And I wouldn't be the least bit surprised if those skates are still there even now.

So, if you go looking for second-hand skates in a used-skate store, you might just get lucky and buy them yourself. I hope that you do. There are three new wishes just waiting for you and I'm sure you could easily think of two without even trying.